Today, Sarah and Duck are getting ready to have some friends round for a sleepover.

Quack!

Greedy Duck!

Not for now!

says Sarah.

Knock! Knock! Knock!

Aha! That must be your first guest, Sarah.

Can you get the door please, Duck?

Quack!

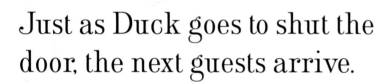

Just as Duck goes to shut the door, the next guests arrive.

Can we come in too?

asks John.

Quack!

Duck nods.

Everyone follows Duck into the kitchen.

So, what's on the cards for this evening, chaps?

That's a **great** idea!

They all sit down in the living room and the game begins.
Eyes down, everyone. Look out for the matching pairs.

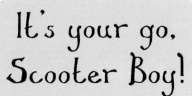

says Sarah.

Now it's Duck's turn . . . then Sarah's . . . now John's.

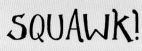

The game goes on . . . and on . . . until . . .

It looks like Flamingo is the winner!

Well, it's quite late. Scooter Boy looks tired.
Maybe it's time for bed?

Duck leads the way as everyone climbs the stairs to get ready for bed.

John unrolls his bed and Scooter Boy sets up his glowing green tent.

Ooo!

Scooter Boy pushes a button on his pyjamas . . .

Watch this!

. . . and they light up!

Time to brush your teeth, chaps?

Ack!

It looks like Duck isn't too keen on having his beak washed!

But then a thoughtful voice comes from the glowing tent.

Do you ever think stickers won't stick any more?

No. Why wouldn't they?

Don't worry. I'm sure they'll all be fine.

Oh, I can't sleep. I'm all awake now!

Oh dear, now **everyone** is awake! Why don't you do something to make yourselves tired again?

I don't think ducks are very good at sleeping on one leg.

Let's try something else.

says Sarah.

Quack!

One day it was getting ready to set . . . sleep . . .

. . . SAIL!

Hmm, feeling tired, Sarah?

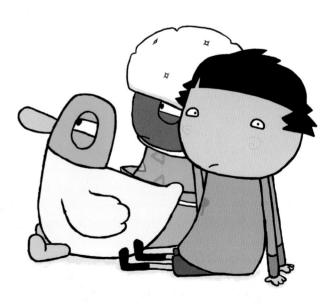

As they go into the technology room, Sarah spots Moon through the window.

Hmm, Moon is awake every night.

Oh yes. Perhaps he can help?

Moon's gentle voice softly explains the ways to fall asleep and
everyone begins

to

feel

very

very

tired.

Well done, Moon.
Everyone is fast asleep!

Goodnight, everyone.

The End